Ten Little FINGERS
and Ten Little TOES

MEM FOX

HELEN OXENBURY

Houghton Mifflin Harcourt Publishing Company

222 Berkeley Street

Boston, MA 02116

Manufactured in China

LEO

4500511925

ISBN 978-0-544-53165-9

For Helena, who teaches them all

—M.F.

For all the babies of the world

—H.O.

There was one little baby
who was born far away.

And another who was born
on the very next day.

And both of these babies,

as everyone knows,

had ten little fingers

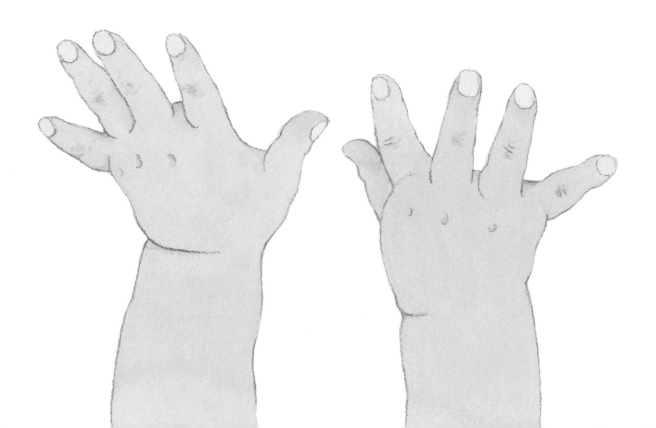

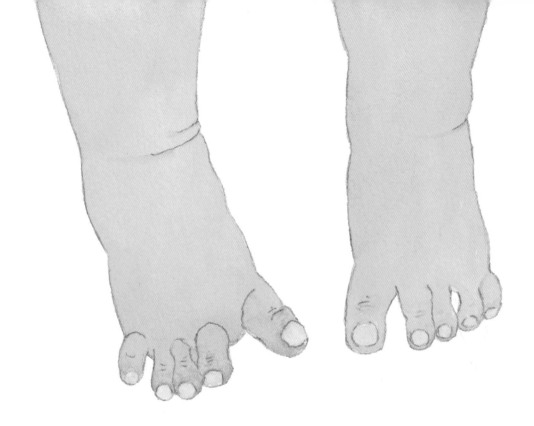

and ten little toes.

There was one little baby who was born in a town.

And another who was wrapped in an eiderdown.

And both of these babies,

as everyone knows,

had ten little fingers

and ten little toes.

There was one little baby
who was born in the hills.

And another who suffered from sneezes and chills.

And both of these babies,

as everyone knows,

had ten little fingers

and ten little toes.

There was one little baby who was born on the ice.

And another in a tent, who was just as nice.

And both of these babies,

as everyone knows,

had ten little fingers

and ten little toes.

But the next baby born was truly divine,
a sweet little child who was mine, all mine.

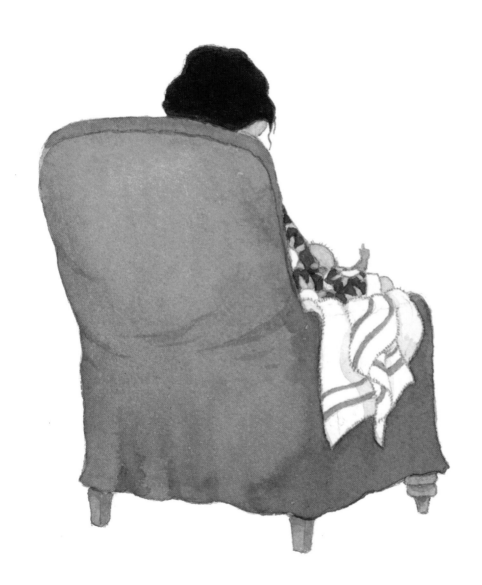

And this little baby,

as everyone knows,

has ten little fingers,

ten little toes,

and three little kisses

on the tip of its nose.